Praise for AC Benus
and the *Secret Melville Series*

The sea has got to Redburn, and good. In that one voyage he's experienced more life in every extreme way than in all his previous years combined. It's got him hooked like a narcotic, but I feel his good nature will serve him well and prevent him from falling into the chasm of hatred and anger that consumed Jackson.
— Stephen *(Redburn)*

The unveiling in this *Typee* gives the reader an extra dimension that readers in Victorian times might have missed (or could very well have understood). Great script, AC!
— J.HunterDunn *(Typee)*

After a conflict between Jarl and An'natu, Redburn comforts Jarl, who breaks down. Their discussion about the bigotry of society is as valid now as it was in Melville's days. It ends with these beautiful words spoken by Redburn:

> "Into the love of equals, we are bound –
> You and I are just alike –
> One to the other, unbroken."

Thanks, AC. Another great script.
— J.HunterDunn *(Omoo)*

You've captured the spirit of Victorian novels quite well – not a jot of happiness anywhere, and conventional morality reigns supreme. Where may we expect to see the workhouse, or the beadle, or grimy smokestack belching out noisome vapors to settle over brick tenement terraces?

More please, and pass the opium so I can have a pleasant dream.
— ColumbusGuy *(Pierre)*

I like symmetry in architecture; music. It has an aesthetic appealing quality. And I find it in *Pierre* as well. Redburn, Emily and Sara make one side of the building, while Pierre, Lucy and Isabelle form the other, completing the symmetrical structure of the whole script.
— J.HunterDunn *(Pierre)*

Praise for AC Benus and
"Becoming Real"

This is a jewel of a short story. There's a type of personal detail given to each of the people in it that makes me think of Somerset Maugham. I love beautiful prose too, and this is written so well that it's a joy to read.

The apple tree sees it all, doesn't it? . . . as it slowly falls apart. But it will bloom again in the spring, and that's the good part.
            —Stephen *(In the Cards)*

What a way to start the journey! I really like how Josh experiences it. As the other reviews before me have pointed out, it's hard to walk away from this chapter without feeling at least one piece of it. Everything this chapter brings up and puts out there is something we can all go and see in reality. That makes the impact even heavier. That night could've gone horribly wrong for Josh in so many ways. Thank goodness it was a good guy who picked him up and showed him around. Very interested to see what the next short story brings.
            —Twisted Dreemz *(The Meeting in the Park)*

I don't think it's fair for you to tell my story so well. However, mine wasn't set in a big city, and it was a bipolar guy who helped me cope. Otherwise, the emotions are identical. Bravo!!!!
            —Cole Matthews *(The Meeting in the Park)*

I am quite fascinated by the power dynamic between younger and older Gay men. Younger queer people generally have a detestable inexperience about them, but their youth is always envied. Older men can use their money and authority to pull rank over younger Gay men, but ultimately, their wisdom is respected. The exchange between Josh and Dick was quite fascinating. I have dated older men and I can totally relate to the events of this chapter. There is a sadness, sometimes, associated with the navigation of the LGBTQ+ world. I hope Josh does not let this deter him or scare him from his journey of finding himself.
            —Bryce Lee *(The Old Man)*

This is so good, so relatable to me it hurts. I am literally cringing as pains pierce my guts reading this. Maybe it's because we are roughly from the same time or maybe our experiences were similar. Regardless, it is so fantastic you have me wincing every paragraph. Brutal and real.
            — Cole Matthews *(The Old Man)*

Also Available from AC Benus

Mojo, a Sex Comedy and Satire
A modern reimagining of Petronius' ancient novel Satyricon *set in Trump's America of conmen, the conned, the ultra-rich, the sexy and the downright silly. "A laugh riot!"*
ebook: ISBN 9781734561074; paperback: ISBN 9781734561050

One Hundred and Fifty-Five Sonnets for Tony
A bold testament to love
ebook: ISBN 9781953389114; paperback: ISBN 9781953389107; hardback: ISBN 9781953389121

Becoming Real: One Coming Out in Seven Short Stories
Setting, St. Louis. Time, 1990 – a young man overcomes the odds
ebook: ISBN 9781953389305; paperback: ISBN 9781953389282; hardback: ISBN 9781953389299

Carême in Brighton, a Culinary Murder Mystery
Mayhem, intrigue and good food at the Prince Regent's seaside villa
ebook: ISBN 9781953389213; paperback: ISBN 9781953389176; hardback: ISBN 9781953389206

Walks With Leporello, an Airedale Remembered
An exploration of Love, God and Dog
ebook: ISBN 9781953389268; paperback: ISBN 9781953389251; hardback: ISBN 9781953389275

Also Available from AC Benus

The Secret Melville Series
  Seven filmscripts based on the sea novels of Herman Melville
    Follow our eponymous hero, from age 19 and his first taste of the
    sea, until he's one of America's most promising writers in New
    York City and its surrounding countryside.

  Volume 1. Secret Melville:
  Redburn & Typee
      ebook: ISBN 9781953389022
      paperback: ISBN 9781953389039

  Volume 2. Secret Melville:
  Omoo & Mardi & Moby-Dick
      ebook: ISBN 9781953389046
      paperback: ISBN 9781953389053

  Volume 3. Secret Melville:
  White-Jacket & Perrie and the Ambiguities
      ebook: ISBN 9781953389060
      paperback: ISBN 9781953389077

Same Love *(Contributor)*
  *Short Story Anthology: a compendium offered during the time of the
  COVID pandemic, D.K. Daniels, Editor*

Poetry Available from AC Benus

Hymenaios, or The Marriage of the God of Marriage
A Classical style myth in 2,600 lines of Blank Verse
ebook: ISBN 9781953389091; paperback: ISBN 9781953389084

Summer 2020 – Hell in a Handbasket
A contender for the Pulitzer Prize in poetry, 2021, this collection
grapples with the year of pandemic, racial injustice and environ-
mental crisis
ebook: ISBN 9781953389015; paperback: ISBN 9781953389008

The Thousandth Regiment
A Translation of and Commentary on Hans Ehrenbaum-Degele's
First World War Poems "Das tausendste Regiment"
ebook: ISBN 1657220583; paperback: ISBN 9781657220584

A Man in a Room, and other poems
Verse following the year when the poet was 21 years old
ebook: ISBN 97817345103; paperback: ISBN 978173456107

The Easiest Thing in the World, and other poems
Marking the third anniversary of the Pulse Nightclub terror attack
ebook: ISBN 9781734561029; paperback: ISBN 9781734561036

Rima Fragmenta, or Fragments of a Rift
Fifty Sonnet for Kevin
ebook: ISBN 9781734561005; paperback: ISBN 9781734561012

First Love: Poems for Ross
For everyone's first love; both bitter and sweet
ebook: ISBN 9781734561081; paperback: ISBN 9781734561098

Poetry Available from AC Benus

Demon Dream
Redemption and shared humanity shine in this retelling of a medieval Japanese legend
ebook: ISBN 9781953389138; paperback: ISBN 9781953389145

Audre Lorde Knows What I Mean – 2021 in Review
A follow-up to Summer 2020, *this collection grapples with the year of the Gop-led Capitol insurrection, racial injustice and the death throes of the environment*
ebook: ISBN 9781953389015; paperback: ISBN 9781953389008

Mikhail Kraminsky, and other poems
Two collections of early poems exploring the pain of youth and being closeted
ebook: ISBN 9781953389152; paperback: ISBN 9781953389169

One Hundred and Fifty-Five Sonnets for Tony
A bold testament to love
ebook: ISBN 9781953389114; paperback: ISBN 9781953389107; hardback: ISBN 9781953389121

Love Looked at Me and Laughed – Poems for Brian
Love is not always easy. Poems to/for/about my first boyfriend
ebook: ISBN 9781953389237; paperback: ISBN 9781953389220
hardback: ISBN 978-1-953389-24-4

Love is Love (Contributor)
Poetry Anthology: In aid of Orlando's Pulse victims and survivors, Lily G. Blunt, Editor, 2016
ebook: ISBN 153514369X; paperback: ISBN 153514369X

AC Benus

Judas Tree

Novella

We have left undone those things
Which we ought to have done;
And we have done those things
We ought not to have done;
And there is no health in us.
 —Book of Common Prayer

I never work better than
when I am inspired by anger –
for when I am angry, I can write,
pray, and preach well.
 —Martin Luther

an AC Benus Impression
San Francisco

Grateful acknowledgement is here offered
for the support and encouragement
I've received on the literary site
www.gayauthors.org.

ISBN 978-1-953389-36-7 (ebook)
ISBN 978-1-953389-35-0 (paperback)

Cover photo:
Pexels.com – Rodnae Productions

Judas Tree
Novella

Part 1: Mary in the Noose

I stand in our 4th grade classroom, alone. The springtime is at my back with open windows, a breeze blowing and occasionally knocking the sticks of the blinds against the aluminum frames. On the air are the voices of the entire school at after-lunch play. The grassy schoolyard is directly in back of those windows behind me, and feeling isolated in this room, I hear the kids' voices – the yelling, the laughing, the sound of running and quick stopping on gravel, and of balls slamming into mitts.

Suddenly a pain tweaks my left elbow. I glance at it. Nothing I can do about it. I shift my feet slightly, looking down to my thin corduroy cuffs. No good. Now a certain stiffness aches in both my shoulders. I take a quick look at the books resting on my extended right arm: 'M' and 'N' weigh down my outstretched palm. I look the other way, and it's worse yet: 'S' and 'T' are an arm's length to my left. I can just crane my head over my shoulder and see the vacant spaces on the bookshelves where four volumes are missing from our class *Word Book Encyclopedia* set.

I know one thing – I think to myself – 'Sister Cornelia in the 3rd grade would never be this evil.' She'd send the other kids out of the room, bend me over her lap and ruler me a few times; over and done with. Miss Hill's novel punishment is meant to be a public disgrace. Anyone passing by the open door can peek in and see me like this. Word will spread about what I did, and they'll all be gossiping about it. But, I won't worry about it now. I'll take my punishment; for what I did, I'll take my due.

It was all a lark anyway. I look up to the ceiling. 'So what if I did it?' I see a couple of pencils stuck up into the dusty, furry coating of the classroom roof. 'It's their fault,' I think. 'Stevie and Dylan, they're the ones who take rubber bands and launch super sharp pencils upwards.' Usually the only effect is, a fine dusting of grayish-white ceiling powder rains down on us kids — asbestos my father calls it. He says it's useful stuff, for fireproofing and the like. But, it was also Stevie who taught Dylan how to tie a hangman's noose. Where Stevie learned to do that — the Boy Scouts? — I don't know. But, Dylan took up the practice and fashioned all the cotton cords of our classroom blinds into mini nooses, neat and tidy. 'So what? So what if I slipped one of them around our classroom's plaster statue of Mary?' It was easy. The wall up to the windows is only half-height, bookcases line the area below; a globe and Madonna live on the shelf at ledge height. 'So? I slipped it around her neck. So? I raised the blind, and took a step back, to see her hanging there. What did it matter?'

She didn't change. The same painted look of pity was on her chalky eyes, which were downcast as always; she pitied the suffering of people and acted like there was nothing she could do about it. Freewill, Monsignor Helfgott told us, the devil is in God's forced gift of freewill — nothing all the sorrow of a virgin mother could do about it, I guess.

From my position, when I'd stepped back with folded arms, I watched her swaying in the slight breeze of this morning's recess, and wondered if she suffered for us, or suffered along with us. I didn't have an answer; what do I know? After all, I'm just a kid.

I was going to lower her. My experiment was over, but something – maybe the devil's voice – said to leave it. I just sat down, pulled out my math book, which was not a likely distraction, and the first person to see it was Maggie, who screamed and ran out of the room.

I sprang to my feet. I undid the holy virgin, but she still did not look up at me; not with accusation, not with anger, but all the while her painted gaze cast a shadow of doubt onto the globe at her feet – the world received her accusations, not me.

Miss Hill stormed in, Maggie just cowering behind her. Mary was back to her usual spot on the shelf, and looked none the worse for the experience. "Simon," my teacher asked very calmly, "why?" I shrugged with a quick glance at the ceiling. "I don't know. No reason."

I shift my weight again. Now the arch of my right foot protests and threatens to cramp. The impulse to charley horse grips my calf and I know I need to relax. There are just ten more minutes, judging by the clock above the door. Relax. But, maybe. Maybe there was something meaningful to what I did this morning. Maybe there was a reason, and I've been feeling – something. I don't know what to call it, but I think it all began a few weeks ago, when I ran into Ralph in the priests' changing room . . . .

Part 2: Warning in the Vestry

"Simon!" Miss Hill snapped. I was looking out the window.

"Yes?"

"Take the rollcall form for this week's funerals to Monsignor Helfgott."

I stood up. I always liked the chance to clear out of the classroom, if only for a few minutes. Believe it or not, Miss Hill consistently finds me to be among the most trustworthy of boys from the 4th grade class, and I enjoy that trust. I grabbed the envelope from my teacher's hand and jetted to the door.

"Come right back," Miss Hill warned.

"Sure thing!" I called from halfway out the door.

I liked going to funerals during the week. For Masses said over those with not much family still around, classes from school were rotated to attend. Masses like these usually started at ten o'clock, and by the time they were over, there'd be only thirty minutes of class before lunch. So, I liked them. In my hand I had this week's roster, and I felt important.

There was no dallying. I went out the door of the glass breezeway that connected the main part of the school – the eight classrooms – to the newer part with library, cafeteria and gym. Immediately out of doors, spring hit me full in the face, and acted like a foot-stamping girl. Sweet scents from the bushes in full flower that crowded the white foundation stones of the church across the street smacked my cheeks and asked where I had been for so long. The side door facing north was grand, and this is where us kids filed in and out for Mass. Between that door and me, a medium-sized tree, the symbol of our town, was in full flower with purplish-red blossoms. The church above the soft blooms was a brick towering giant with stained glass and multi-colored plaster and paint inside and out. Built in 1894, Saint Lazarus himself has a special niche for his statue. It's inside at the back and next to the main doors. Mary, his companion, has her own niche on the other side of the entry. In front of them, metal stands glow and flicker with tall glass votives. We learned that the parish priest made these with his own two hands when the church was still under construction. I guess he wanted a permanent place in his parish. With these candles, I like to light one for both the mother, and then the friend of Jesus – when I have a spare 20¢, that is.

The church loomed in front of me, at least the backside did. The front, with the spire, was on the street removed by one block from the school. I glanced around, sucking in the fresh air, but there was no opportunity to dally here, not in the open. Sister Cornelia and the 3rd grade classroom, and Miss Wagstaff and her 1st grade classroom, face this street and have a full view of me crossing over to the church. I went up to the back door, the smaller door on the south side of the church that no worshiper should use, because it puts you into the vestry, or the priests' changing room. Monsignor Helfgott's modern house is connected here to the old church by a breezeway, like the one at school, but I preferred to come into the church, especially the vestry.

I stopped once I was inside. Behind me, the great wooden door slowly closed and made a clicking sound as the latch engaged. The light contrast was terrific, and as my eyes adjusted from full sunlight to the dampened bluish stained glass-lit space, my nostrils greedily took in the smell of peace: peaceful incense. I always think of that fragrance as peaceful – its powder-burn singed my nose for a moment – it seemed to my sense of smell as strong as the sunlight just shut out had been to my eyes.

Now I could blink and see. Straight in front of me, about twenty-five feet, the door out of the vestry to the connecting breezeway was closed. It was quiet. I glanced up to the starry blue and gold windows along the plain, outer wall, then over to the objects of my investigation. For the other three walls were lined oaken closets; some open to the room; some sealed with carved doors; all intricate with gothic arches and flourishes. Again, I listened. No sounds. I stepped over to an open cabinet, and with a quick glance at the pale blue ceiling – vaulted and painted with silver and gold stars, I extended my hand and slowly walked along the vestments. I could feel the white silk 'damask' – as my mother had taught me to call it – and heavier fabrics, all with gold stitching that made them feel more like drapery than clothes. With each slight pressure, my fingertips seemed to release deeper ruffles of scent, and these two sensations combined to swoon my senses. In the next cabinet were coarser feelings – lightweight linens, scratchy wools, and there tucked at the end, sackcloth. A sandpaper jute, meant only for Ash Wednesday, it shocked my touch of it. I imagined it smelled like the biting smudge the Monsignor smeared on my forehead once a year; the smell of regret.

What was that? I froze. Somewhere, a door slammed. Somewhere, tennis shoes were running on a protesting marble floor. Was it coming closer? The footfall grew louder.

The door from the breezeway stuttered open with force. I wanted to melt into the vestments. A slight step back, and I could have made it, into and behind them . . . .

Now I could see. Running halfway through the vestry to the outer door was Ralph, a kid in the 6th grade – a freckled redheaded boy who always made me think of him as a male version of the Wendy's hamburger girl.

For a moment, I thought he would continue and run straight out to the sunshine and spring morning, but for some reason he stopped. The door he had just pummeled creaked closed, and in painful silence, he stood there and listened to it latch behind him. He stood stock still, and as if in slow motion, raised his open palms up to his eyes — his eyes, which were wild looking and frightening. In an instant, he sobbed. It was a harsh, guttural moan, and those hands went up and struck his none-too handsome face — but his sob was cut short — he saw me.

"I—" I tried to explain, walking along the clothes towards the outer door. But he instantly sprang, like a kid *Rock 'em Sock 'em* toy boxer, and he grabbed my arm.

I did not want to look into his eyes, but I couldn't help it, they were everywhere.

"What are you doing here?!" he demanded, his tears getting wiped by the back of his free hand. There was something bitter, something acrid on his breath. I turned away from his spittle.

"I have to deliver this"—I was holding up the envelope—"to Monsignor Helfgott."

"Look . . . " Now he grabbed me by both arms. He jostled me until I was forced to lock my eyes on his. "I know you're a good kid, and that you will listen to me. *OKAY?*"

His desperate attempt to sound reasonable was terrifying.

"Yeah," I said.

Snot began to leak out of one of his nostrils. His tears fell freely now with nothing but my sweater and slacks to stop them, and the crack in his voice became hoarse.

"Never — I mean *never,*" he choked out, "let yourself be alone with Monsignor Helfgott." He continued more softly, like he was trying to connect with my soul, but that voice, his breath, and those eyes, they all were scary. "Do you under-stand me?"

My hesitation apparently goaded him, for he shook me violently. He raised his voice so that the plaster ceiling vaults pinged in frightening reverberations. "Do you *UNDERSTAND ME?!*" His glare demanded that I answer him.

No. I did not. But, I nodded. And I must have looked as afraid as I felt, for in a moment he blinked at me, and some shadow of a deep and pained pity seemed to wake him up. He slowly released his grip, and it felt like I sank down a couple of inches to settle back onto the floor, so tense had my spine become. I swallowed hard and watched as Ralph returned to his position halfway between the doors. His back was towards me; his hands went up and locked fingers on top of his head as if he were debating something. After a pregnant moment, he spun around. He held eyes on mine as he wiped the snot and tears from his mouth and cheeks. Then he changed, and with some kind of calmness, could tuck his shirttails into his slacks. I hadn't even noticed they were out till that moment.

"Give me that," he said, holding out his hand towards my envelope. A different kind of peacefulness, perhaps a hard-won resolution, was now in his voice. "I'll give it to him," he said strongly.

I held up the envelope and took a step towards him, but then I stopped. We both heard it – the sound of grownup shoes on the floor of the breezeway. As if in slow motion, Ralph turned back to me with some unspeakable terror on his face, one that quietly formed into a look of compassion, of disappointment, of shame – I didn't know which – but it was for me, and me alone. As I came up to the guy, Ralph bolted through the exterior door. He left me there, facing the burning sunlight, while behind me, the breezeway door unclicked, and I could hear Monsignor Helfgott's voice call out "Ralphie!"

I turned to face him. The heavy outer door crept up to put pressure on my back and lock. I wondered why I should not be alone with this man.

Part 3: Judas Tree

We sat at his dining room table. Monsignor Helfgott looked at me very intently. I liked our priest. I liked his homilies – always about being a better, more selfless person. His standby sermon was on the dangers of the 'Big I' – as he called it. The tendency to think only about myself, or the *Big I*, before considering how others feel, or what kind of damage the *Big I* could do to them. I liked him because his lessons always came around to our duty to love one another as ourselves.

"You're Simon? Right – 4th grade?"

"Yes, sir." I was pleased to be on his radar. "In Miss Hill's class," I added helpfully.

"Good. Um – would you like some milk?"

"Um . . . " I considered it. "It's almost lunchtime. I can wait."

Monsignor Helfgott's gaze at me turned momentarily severe, but it faded back instantly as he said, "Ralphie was upset. Did he say . . . why?"

"No, I—"

"Oh, don't concern yourself about it. I'll find out later."

I shrugged. "I've never seen a boy like that, like Ralph, cry before. I guess he was in pain—"

He cut me off. "I said I'll take care of Ralph. Now – what about you? I know Stevie and Dylan from your class are altar boys, and have been for a couple of years, so why not you? Don't you like church?"

"Oh, I do, sir. I really do. But, my folks don't get up on Sunday mornings. *So . . .* I can't be an altar boy."

"Hmm – they should come to church, you know."

"They know."

"Well, do you like your religion class?"

"Yes, sir."

Now he was distracted, looking out the window and towards the school. But he asked, "Can you tell me the legend of your town's name?"

"Judas Tree?"

"Yes." He turned moist eyes on mine. "Yes, the Judas tree legend."

I puffed up, sat bolt upright on his wooden dining room chair, for this was one I knew by heart. "A mighty tree grew in Jerusalem. In the springtime when our Lord was crucified, this tree and all of its kind around the world – including here – bloomed in pure-white buds. Judas, remorseful at betraying Jesus with a kiss, threw a rope over the sturdy tree in Jerusalem, tied it off and hung himself. At the moment he died for his sins, the tree grew weak and feeble – its mighty limbs shriveled to mere sticks, and all the pure-white blossoms became stained in his blood. Every tree all around the world – including here – only grew to a small size and bloomed red with the disgrace of his crime. Like the one outside the church door is blooming now."

Did it look like Monsignor Helfgott was going to cry too . . . but, again, it passed.

"Good," he said while swallowing. "It's true. But, I can teach you more – if you are interested . . . . "

"Yes." I pulled up to the edge of my chair, arms just before the elbows on the table. Something sad reached him. He put his hand out and touched the top of mine.

"You know the story well, but do you know where the Judas tree was? Why he selected that one tree, out of all the others?"

I was amazed. I had no idea there was such a 'why.' I shook my head.

"Because, that tree grew in front of the tombs of the high priests, the ones who wanted Jesus arrested. See, they had betrayed Judas. They had promised him that Jesus would not go to the Romans, but stay with the priests." His moist hand clamped onto mine. "Do you see why he chose that tree?"

My mouth went slack. I shook my head.

"Jewish purity laws forbid death, especially suicidal death, from anywhere near holy places. The priests' tombs were holy . . . until—"

"Judas ruined it for them."

"Yes." He squinted a smile. He was relieved to see I understood. He let go and patted the top of my hand.

"Yes. Judas Iscariot betrayed those who had betrayed Jesus."

"Do you think . . . " I hated to ask him.

"Do I think, what?"

"Judas is in Hell?"

"The Church says he is, therefore, we must think of Judas in Hell. But – I wonder, and maybe you wonder too – if Christ is all love, and he needed Judas to complete his mission here on Earth, among us, then can a person of all love punish a redeeming act of love?"

His eyes drifted back to the school, and I thought I better get a note explaining my absence to Miss Hill.

"Do you see, Simon? Only God was with him on that tree. Only God knows if Judas made a perfect Act of Contrition – only God knows what was on his dying lips, or what was deep in his heart at its last beating." He gripped my hand again, this time with a clammy force that made me want to pull back, but I didn't. "I wonder, son, if you've ever made a mistake—" He corrected himself with a headshake. "Mistakes."

I didn't think we were talking about religion anymore, so I asked, "Like a sin?"

He slowly let go of my hand. "Yes. A sin . . . . "

I went slack-jawed. I wondered if – or how – he found out about my little 'habit.' It was time to come clean. "Well, sir," I started. "I sometimes, not all the time, sir, light more than one votive candle for my dime . . . " I trailed off, slouched my head and spine and withdrew my hands into my lap.

"Listen to me." He leaned across the table and put a finger under my chin, raising it. I was starting to see there *were* tears in his eyes. "Doing something wrong can only be proportional to the depth of devotion of one's faith."

I bit my lip. I didn't understand.

He stood and wiped his tears with a white hankie from his inner coat pocket. He paced between my chair and the window. He went on, "A deep betrayal of a lightly held belief is a light sin. A light betrayal of a deeply held faith is a great sin – a great mistake." From the window, he swallowed hard and tried to smile at me. "You lit the extra candles in the expression of the goodness within you. It's as if you lit them knowing – understanding – that others, perhaps of a lesser faith, would see them as examples of the flames that can kindle goodness in *all* who see them – who make of them tokens of God's love for us; of his protection over us." He walked behind my chair, and now he laughed. "You will pay the dimes you owe, in good time. Don't concern yourself about that. Do you follow?"

I nodded. I smiled. I thought I did understand. I brought goodness into the world by being good – that, and that alone. Standing at the window, I could see his face darken in profile, and a gray circle of light hover over his salt and pepper head.

He said, sounding like when he offered a prayer, "I hope your life is only full of mistakes like the ones you've made so far." He raised an arm and leaned against the frame with an elbow. Towards the school, he murmured, "There are other mistakes too heavy to bear. Ones that further darkness in the world, ones that hand over the safety placed in our hands, for the greater the trust, the greater the treachery."

His head pivoted to me, but his glance this time was weird. I did not follow him now, but something in his manner made me ask, "You mean, a mistake like Judas made?"

He inhaled sharply, and his form crumpled before me. He kneeled at the side of my chair, and I heard a faint choking sound, even though his mouth was closed. He slowly raised one hand, and I could feel his moist palm stroke my short blond crew cut. With his other, he turned his knuckles in and ran the short ends of his fingers over my cheek.

"Yes, son – a mistake like Judas made – a betrayal of love like Judas made."

His closeness brought a wave of incense to my brain. It rose from the folds of his clothes and let me think of nothing else. His nearness, the holy smell rising from him, stilled me, even though I could not help but feel afraid. None of this was right. None of it made much sense. Even the familiar – even the good – seemed suspect. And his eyes, the eyes of my priest, appeared wild. They were pleading with me, showing just as much fear, just as much pain – and perhaps something unknowable, like shame – as I had seen in the vestry, in the wild eyes of poor Ralphie.

🝆   🝆   🝆

Walking out of the vestry door, the spring sunshine was dimmed by gathering clouds overhead. To the west, behind Saint Lazarus School, tinges of gray edged the horizon. As I walked across the street, I fingered Monsignor Helfgott's note and thought about how much I like attending Mass. I liked squinting my eyes at the candlelight, and blurring the pinpoints of brightness into glowing diffused halos. It seemed magical to do so, and turn the flames sitting above the back and front altars into visions of the Holy Spirit Itself. I loved the Benediction; the waft of perfumed smoke from the censer kicked by the priest's hands back and forth around the altar and over the heads of us worshipers. And I loved the Host in the monstrance shown to us while Stevie or Dylan, or one of the other altar boys, picked up the sacryn – the brass hand bells. Some boys would curtly jostle the bells and quickly stifle them afterwards. Some others would shake and shake, too long making a magical presence sustained to be mystical anymore. But there were other boys who know – yes, I think Ralph is one such boy. Ralph would gently pick up the sacryn, and start soft, heavenly ringing with the bareness of slow reverberations, and then, as the Monsignor raised the sacred, the blessed, Host of the body of Christ above his head, Ralph would increase tempo and volume to subtle heights – all of this, all of it, let down just as quietly, so that by the end of the Benediction, "It is right to praise the Lord" is echoed from the beginning of the prayer in meaningful silence.

I stopped on the sidewalk. Something like a realization hit me. I was three feet from the school breezeway door. That's right. I remembered in 2nd grade, just after Stevie and Dylan became altar boys, I had heard them talking. The older altar boys, Dylan told Stevie, said to always be in pairs when with Monsignor Helfgott. "Always in pairs equals never alone," I murmured. The loneliness this memory generated reminded me of the feeling I got walking through peoples' yards. I was warned against that too, but in 2nd grade, I did it anyway.

Something made me feel sick to my stomach about that old man's folding chair. I had met him, doing what I was not supposed to do, and I felt then as I feel now, like a dark shadow was creeping over me.

Part 4: Like Adam and Eve

Sidewalks are so boring – always the same – same pavement, light poles, mailboxes and sewer grates. But, to venture off through the green grass – to set off like a great space explorer through the beckoning unknown – that enlivened a simple task, like walking home, to the status of adventure. It's only about three or four small-town blocks from school to Willetta's house – the house of the family that takes care of me before and after classroom hours – until my mom picks me up after work. I'd cross the open space behind Judas Tree's public high school, which was a huge field, and plunge into the quiet streets of look-alike houses. When alone, I'd pick a likely house, and keeping my bearings, walk boldly along their property line into their backyard. From there I'd assess the best way to pass into an adjoining yard, mindful of fence and dog – which were few – and emerge one block closer to my destination. I didn't do this every day. I did not do this for long, mainly because people observed me and called around in a game of grown-up tattletale to find out who I was, so I could be warned not to do that. A couple of houses I avoided because voices would call out from windows. From one such house, a crotchety old man yelled from his tiny bathroom window – but on the second trip around, on another day, this 'old man' turned out to be a pimply teenager who couldn't help laughing loudly with a couple of his buddies – all cramped at that bathroom window to try and scare me.

But there was one exception to those who remained indoors. A kindly man with slow gait and white hair hailed me on my second or third trip over his property. By this time I was more cautious, because Willetta, my host mom, had taken me aside, and with intensity told me one of the neighbors called. I did not deny walking a different path, but she told me to stop. My "Why?" could not be answered – Willetta made only vague reference to 'bad people' – so I went about my very occasional forays with greater stealth, so she wouldn't be burdened with the hearing of them. The lure of grass and trees was too strong. But then this white-haired man greeted me.

At first I thought he was angry. I quick-turned to walk back down his driveway to the sidewalk, but in a moment he was at my side.

"What's your name?" he asked with grinning voice.

I stammered, "I'm sorry . . . sir. I'll be . . . going—"

"Nonsense," he said, and put a fatherly hand on my shoulder. "Come and sit a spell." Turning me around, and walking me back along the side of his house, he added, "Now. What's your name?"

"Simon."

"Well. Nice to meet you, Simon. You can call me Allen, all right?"

I nodded. His warm smile put me at ease. I was making a friend.

As Allen passed a screened window, he turned and called into the house, "Mother, we've got a guest."

By the time Allen and I arrived in his backyard – I was familiar with it: a concrete patio, a line of blue spruce along the back, no dog – his white-haired wife was coming out the back door. She was brushing down her frilly-edged apron and patting down her hair.

"This is Simon. He's going to set a spell," Allen told her.

"Oh, you boys want some lemonade?" She tossed the question expectantly between Allen and me.

"Yes. Good idea, Mother," Allen said with eager smiles at me.

She disappeared and Allen went to the side of his patio and stooped down. "Help me with these," he said over his shoulder.

I went up to him, and he put a folding aluminum chair with green mesh webbing in my hands. I opened it as he set up a little table and a chair for himself.

"Well, heaven's sake – Sit down, take a load off." He motioned the action to me with open palms.

I did sit, and we looked out on to the quiet afternoon of his grass and grown-up trees. I had favored Allen's yard because I liked spruce. We have one at home, and in clumps, as in Allen's yard, I could get myself into the dark recesses and feel safe and unseen; somehow feel primitive and connected. I'd feel that way until the sap or the sharp needles would prod me to be on my way.

A robin appeared and hopped across the lawn.

"You go to Saint Lazarus – Right?"

"Yes, how do you know?"

"Oh"—he deflected any serious air with his smile—"I asked around."

Allen and I sat there a tranquil moment or two. The screen door opened and a tray with pitcher and two glasses led 'Mother's' way.

"Here we go, boys." And she set it down. Immediately, Allen poured me a juice glass of pale lemonade and put it into my grip. As I sipped my first sweet-tart mouthful, Mother put hands on hips and made an odd expression to Allen. He made some quick gesture, like a flick of his fingers at her.

"Well," Mother called out. "I know you boys want to talk." And she left us.

Allen sipped and rocked back on his seat. I copied him, feeling the warm spring afternoon overtake us, leading us to a peaceful state. In fact, I felt happy, like I was wanting for nothing.

"So . . . " said Allen quietly. "You like pictures?"

"Pictures?" I shrugged. "Sure. What kind of pictures?"

"Well, you see"—he leaned over to my chair, and I instinctively leaned in to receive his confidence—"down in the basement, I've got quite a collection of pictures. If you want to see them." Then he added reassuringly, "Mother never goes down there. She'll leave us alone." Looking around as if some super-secret thing was about to be passed to me, he said, "You like looking at naked men . . . and women . . . ?"

I said the first thing that came to mind. "You mean, like Adam and Eve?"

Some cloud passed over Allen's face. It puzzled me a moment. It looked like he was waking from a bad dream, but in a second, it cleared and something like the old smile returned.

"Yes, Simon – like Adam and Eve – in the garden, all alone." He leaned back and sipped his lemonade. With half-a-glance back to me, he casually asked, "So, you want to see them?" Then he gently warned, "You must tell no one."

"No . . . " I put my drink down. "I have to get to Willetta's house. I'm already late. I don't want her to find out I've been walking through yards again."

I stood up.

Nonplussed, Allen stood too. "Yes. It's best if you go back along the sidewalk – But, if you come back tomorrow, I can take you down into the basement." Again he offered a confidence, and bent it directly into my ear, "And you can see naked boys and girls."

Something of a thrill passed through my spine. A strong twitch of curiosity made me tell Allen, "Okay."

Now Allen's face was flooded with smiles. He put his arm around the back of my shoulders and walked me down his driveway. At the sidewalk, he turned me to face his serious eyes.

"You won't tell anyone, right? This is just between us friends; it's between you and me. Right?"

I nodded, but something had changed about Allen. His look of a friend now cast a dark shadow across his eyes. Maybe it was just the way the springtime sun was back over his white hair, but something looked different.

"See you tomorrow," I said, and hoisted my bookbag over my shoulder. I walked down the sidewalk, and at the corner, turned back to see Allen still in front of his home. He waved at me. I waved back and went on to Willetta's house.

The next twenty-four hours, every time I thought of Allen, the warm expression he had for me, the calm and stillness of the setting within his yard, and his niceness, I felt little prickles of something move along my spine. I kept imagining his basement. What would it be like, this place never seen by his wife, presumably, not by any woman, where just 'us boys' were allowed to go. Would this basement be full of shelves, each shelf stacked with photo albums, like the kind my mom kept? Would he sit me at a table, a bare bulb over the open book he set in front of me? Black and white snapshots – what would the naked people be doing? And over and over, I heard Allen's near-whisper of a voice " . . . naked boys and girls . . . . "

To say I was curious would be an understatement, and all day, when I thought about the folding chair, the blue spruce, and the tart sting of the lemonade, that prickly sensation would rise and fall and seem to settle in the lowest part of my back – from there, it would move front to center, then back to the rear again – and as this tingle crept, I slowly grew nervous.

Leaving school that afternoon, I had every intention of going to Allen's house. I could see the scene – sitting out, the clump fortress of spruce in the background, a robin arrives, we go to his basement, creaky steps, the table, a chair – the pictures – then what? That I could not see.

As I approached the street to turn towards his house, I stopped. A voice in the back of my head, an insistent voice, said 'No.' It was not right.

I ran all the rest of the way to Willetta's house, and I never walked through any yards after that. I did keep my word to Allen though, and never told anyone.

The charley horse impulse in my right calf had lessened. Now the encyclopedia letters become heavier with each passing moment. I sneer – Miss Hill won't win. This punishment is meaningless – just like the action I am being punished for. Better not think about the weight of the books – but is it better to go on with my train of thought?

I never walked on Allen's street again. The two years from now back to then might be two centuries, as distant as it feels. My strongest sight is of those cloudy eyes at our parting. My strongest thought about the event is some shade of shame. No one ever knew. Not Willetta, not my mom, not Monsignor Helfgott, who I might have told in Confession – but why? I hadn't done anything wrong. I hadn't done anything at all. But now, my chief wonder was at Allen's collection of 'naked boys and girls.' Where did he get such pictures? It meant that other boys like me, and girls too, had been with him, or with others with a camera – it was too much to dwell on – other than to wonder how many kids had actually seen Allen's basement.

I shift weight on my feet. I sigh loudly. I desperately want other things to think about. And then, the meeting in memory of photos and trees soothes me into thinking about the one person I feel is a true thick-and-thin friend to me. But he is gone.

Suddenly, for no reason, I am overcome with sadness. I think of Jake. I think of his wild brother, Jeremy, and how rotten it is that they moved away. Visiting them on their grandmother's farm was the best thing in my life. Now each time we go there – my dad driving along the bluff roads, windows down, him enjoying the trees and hills and clouds as much as me – it will never mean the same thing again. The destination was changed, even though I was going to the same place. If Jake was not there, it was not the same.

Yet, all in all, I couldn't help but crack up to think of when we first met, and of their grandmother's beautiful dog – a red-haired gentleman of a hound with a special trick he had taught himself.

Part 5: The Smiling Setter

When my dad told me we were going to visit Flo, a good customer of his antique shop, I never expected to encounter all that I did. His '76 Ford pickup rattled an old wooden bridge that had warning signs about no more than two tons on it at a time, but on the other side, far from Judas Tree, through miles of bluff roads with craggy heights and soft green willows and hickory, was this ancient floodplain of the Mississippi, and black-earth farmland.

My dad said over the road rumble, "See the bluffs over there?" He gestured out my side window, to the west. About five miles off were the misty-blue hills I knew to be across the river in Missouri. 'Those," he said, "used to be the far bank of the river." Grinning at me, he nevertheless gripped the wheel tighter as we jostled into and then out again of a gravel pothole. "The near bank"—he pointed behind us—"was right here! Come the end of the ice age, the river was five miles wide."

"Whoa!" I said, and meant it.

We passed by a neat and tidy farmhouse set back a good quarter-mile from the road. Some shade trees grew along the back three sides, but the house stood aloof of them, and looked like an old wooden toy block, so perfectly formed was it; this farm belonged to the Durham family. Driving past their homestead, somehow, anticipation grew, and at the next driveway after the blockhouse, after the two-ton bridge, our light blue Ford turned. A long gravel drive curved past an old white farmhouse that was nearest the road, past a giant tree growing behind the house, and off to a barn on the right-hand side. As my dad slowly steered and listened to his tires crunching gravel, I looked across this barn. It was not the usual dairy or hay barn. The whole thing was covered in new buff-colored aluminum siding, and at ground level, modern windows looked out with lace curtains tucked behind.

As the truck stopped, a woman came out of the barn's back door. She was thin and animated, and around her heels with loving looks up into her face was a gorgeous dog. My dad waved to the woman through the windshield, looking like John Wayne – reserved, not too eager – and we stepped out into the summer's day.

"Ed!" the woman called out. My focus was on the dog, but I saw my dad hike his waistband, and the adults greeted each other.

The dog ran to my dad, lowered his ears and head and wagged invitingly. But, my dad ignored him. Then the dog saw me. Up he came, and his back rose to my mid-chest level. He sidled me, sticking his back flank against my tummy, and with lolling tongue, glanced back at me. Of course, I petted him and he liked it. I suppose he liked me as much as I liked him. This type of dog I had not seen before. He had long straight red hair fringing all down his sides and legs, a low and flat dome between his ears, and he had big brown Bambi eyes to look at me with.

"My little helper." My dad slapped my shoulder and startled me.

"How do? I'm Flo."

"Simon." I shook her offered hand.

"And that"—she beamed—"is Rex." Then to the dog she said, "Aren't you, Rex? Such a good boy . . . " Rex went into ecstatics and turned a wet nuzzle into my raised palms.

I looked into Flo's eyes. She was in her early 60s, same as my dad, and there was only goodness and generosity in her heart. That I could tell in an instant.

"What kind of dog is that?" I asked her.

"Irish Setter," she told me proudly.

In the near distance I heard a screen door slam, and the light sound of gravel being run upon.

Flo explained to my dad, "My daughter lives in the house with her husband." Then she added to me, "And – they have two little boys, both around your age." No sooner had she said this than the two boys in question came running up. Flo went on, mussing their hair for identification, "This is Jeremy; he's eight. And this is Jake; he's twelve. How old are you, son?"

"I'm ten."

I eyed the boys. They eyed me back. They both had long brown hair – at least longer than my blond crewcut – and wore jeans and tee-shirts with some team logos on them. Jake's was yellow, with black letters; Jeremy's was a Cardinal's shirt. I was a bit jealous because my mom never let me wear tee-shirts with anything written on them. She also never let me wear just a tee-shirt; always something over it – but – oh, well.

"Let's give them a tour," Flo said to her grandsons.

"Oh – Boring!" Jeremy said, throwing his arms full in the air and lolling his head around. "Not me . . . . " He then ran off to play.

"I'll go, Grandma." Jake said, and Flo squeezed him by the shoulder into her tummy for a moment, lifting Jake on one foot for balance. As she released him, Jake passed an embarrassed smile to me and shoved his hands in his jean pockets. It's nice, I thought to be well-loved, and I could tell the boys were loved well by Flo.

And off we went. First, we went around our truck to look at the land. Behind the white house was an immense tree of some weird willow-type. Forty-foot tall with dark heart-shaped leaves and great drooping pods, it was mysterious.

Then we went through the first level of the barn — garage, kitchen, and to the unused front door entering into the dining room and living room combination. This last room alone was about as big as the section of my school housing grades one through four. Back through the garage, Flo paused at the bottom of a flight of steps. "Now, we'll go see the loft — and my collections." She had intoned this with an air of wonder to my dad and me. Everyone went up ahead of me, except Jake, and when we got to the landing, it was dark. The adults had moved off a few steps somewhere, and I stood, sensing — with nothing relating to sight or smell or sound — that something cavernous lay right in front of me. It seemed as if the vastness of a church cut off from its windows was but a step beyond, though there was nothing to give it away, except the incredible pressure perceived from a void — a holy feeling. Jake moved from behind me, coming to stand next to me after mounting the last step, and it seemed for a moment I could feel his pulse with mine; he was expecting something great to happen too. Though he should know what he might see, something else, like a connection, was charged in the air between us, and it thrilled me. Neither of us moved, and then a loud switch was thrown, and dazzling light flooded. My dad and Flo moved into the open space a bit, but I stood where I was — transfixed.

Above me, a ceiling of barn beams rose twenty-five feet, left exposed and contrasting sharply with acres of white plaster between. The whole loft was open below these arched interlinking hands with every outer wall lined in cabinets — old ones, new ones, many with glass shelves, and all of them lit.

The contents glimmered – art glass of many hues and descriptions, racks of cut crystal, paste-white porcelain, fancy painted German table china, and so forth, and so on and on. The open space of the floor between the cabinets was artfully mazed with antique tables and desks, glass display cases, and here and there, floor lamps, birdcages and statues on pedestals. Each case, every desk and tabletop, was full to the brim with carefully sorted exquisits of every variety. This one room looked like a private museum of the best taste, or an amazing secret department store of antiques.

I must have been slack-jawed or something, because next thing I knew, Jake was knocking me with his elbow. He leaned his upper arm against my shoulder, and bent towards me. I looked into his grinning smile, and he closed in on my ear.

"I know," he whispered in suppressed excitement. "I like it up here too." The skin of his forearm brushed against mine with warmth.

Seeing his face like this, hearing his voice like that, it seemed I was looking in some kind of mirror; hearing my own voice speak to me. Not as I was, but what I was to be in a couple of years. I too felt a thrill, and I laughed a little. I couldn't help it.

After the tour, we were back in Flo's kitchen. Above the sink, a deep shelf below a window looked out on my dad's truck. On it were green plastic pots bursting over with pointy cactus – aloe vera, Flo would later teach me, good for cuts – but right in the center of the shelf, glistening in the sunlight was a glass pitcher. It looked weird. New, not an antique, with a bulbous base circled with big acid-yellow sunflowers, and a brown liquid filling it.

Flo was at the refrigerator. There was a loud clack of ice in glasses. "You boys want Sun Tea?"

"Sure," Jake called out with gusto. I didn't know what she meant, but in a moment, she picked up the sunflower pitcher and filled an array of glasses on the table.

"Sit!" Flo told my dad, and he did with his typical half-grunt of relief. Flo put frigid and sweating glasses in the greedy hands of Jake and me. Flo sat down and poured a big glass for my dad, saying to her side, "After your tea, you boys should go out and play with your brother."

I brought the glass to my lips, locking eyes on Jake, wondering what 'Sun Tea' was going to taste like. Jake chuckled a moment. I must have looked disappointed. It tasted like tea to me – oh, well – I drank it all. Soon, Jake put his glass down with a thump and motioned for me to follow him. Out the screen door we went, careful to keep Rex inside. Jake nodded and started jogging towards the farmhouse. I sprinted with him.

I could hear two small dogs yapping along with Jeremy's voice as he played with a tall sick. We came up to the giant tree and saw him using the stick to whack at pods on the lower branches. They fell, and the two small dogs – who I hadn't seen before – ran around with eyes skyward. One dog was all white, just a tip of tan on one ear, and the other was mottled in dark gray-brown.

"What'cha doing?" Jake called out.

"Collecting cigars," his brother called back, whatever that was supposed to mean.

Jeremy dropped his stick and ran straight up to me. "Let's play Star Wars!" And instantly, he held out his hands like he was gripping something. He sent one foot back to brace himself.

"Play, what?" I asked.

"Star Wars!" Jeremy shouted.

I looked at Jake, lost. Jake explained, "It's a new movie out this summer – about space fighters."

Now I was excited, and asked, "You mean, like Space: 1999? I love Space: 1999!"

"Better!" Jeremy now swung his arms and started making whooshing sounds with his mouth. "It's about fighting with laser swords! Come on!" I mimicked his stance and soon I was making whooshing sounds too. Jeremy and I fought our way halfway around the white farmhouse, and then halfway around the barn, with the dogs and Jake in tow.

Later, the three of us were pooped and lay in the grass with hands behind our heads. We looked up at the clouds.

"That one," I said pointing. "That's a squirrel with a big fat walnut." I turned my head to Jake next to me. "See?"

"Well – maybe . . . " Jake cocked his head at the sky.

"That one," Jeremy cried out, "looks like Big Bird."

"Where?" Jake and I said together.

"There!" Jeremy pointed with his full arm.

"My God – you're right!" I exclaimed. When I glanced at Jake for confirmation, he was laughing, but I don't know at what.

After a quiet pause, Jeremy asked me in all seriousness, "You ever stop a fan blade with your fingers?"

"No," I said. "That's dangerous." I pictured my dad's old Emerson oscillating fan with the brass blades. That thing goes a million miles an hour.

"Dangerous . . . ? Wanna bet?" Jeremy propped up on one elbow.

I knit my brows. "Bet, what?"

"Bet a quarter that I can stop a moving fan blade with my fingers."

With deflecting laughter, I tried to say, "I don't think you should—"

Jake interrupted. "We know how," the older brother chimed in with reassurance. "Don't worry, Simon."

"Come on!" Jeremy stood. "I'll show you!"

In a moment, we were up and jogging to the farmhouse. The back part, closest to the tree, was a large screened-in-porch. We went in. A big modern box fan with plastic blades and covers was sitting on a table. Jeremy went over to it and popped off the closely spaced grill.

Jeremy said proudly, "Now, watch this." Jake and I gathered next to him. Jeremy turned on the fan, and air rushed into our faces and pushed our shirts against our tummies and chests.

Jeremy raised his eyebrows a moment, and then made a determined grin. He slowly brought his right hand, with extended fingers, towards the whirling blades. I thought that when they were spinning, the blades looked like one big meat grinder. He paused, then drove his fingers in. For a moment, the fan motor protested with a muffled whine, and the blades slapped Jeremy's fingers over and over. But the instant after that, the blades were still, with Jeremy's fingers pressing on one of the blade section near the hub.

"See!" He beamed and pulled his hand away. We were again pelted with air.

I turned to Jake, my words cut up by the fan. "Your brother's crazy!" And I made my point with a loco motion around my temple.

Without a word, Jake stepped past me, and Jeremy stood aside. The older brother did the same maneuver, and then smiled warmly at me. As he let go, his chopped words came up to dare me. "Now, you try."

Laughing, I tried to stall. "I . . . " I knew my dad would kill me if he found out.

Over the whir of the motor, Jake told me frankly, "If you want to hang out with us, you have to do what we do."

"Yeah!" Jeremy chimed.

But then Jake reached out and put his grip around my wrist. He was firm, but used just enough pressure to compel me to his side. When there, he said into my ear, "Just try. I *know* you can do it."

I nodded.

"Put your fingers out stiff." Jake lifted my hand, showing me. "Only approach from this angle." He used my fingers to point in the direction the blades were moving.

I straightened my spine. Jake and Jeremy moved to the front and were pressed by the wind. I bit my lip and dove in.

The sting of the blades slapping my fingers was momentarily numbing, but I pressed down and the blade came under my control.

I looked at the brothers with jubilant disbelief. They lit up, and Jake quickly came over to switch the fan off. He crooned in my ear, "Now, you are one of us." As he pulled away, again, I couldn't help but laugh at that odd mirror-effect that made me feel important, that made me feel connected.

"Yeah!" Jeremy sang out. *"We're* crazy!"

While I was thinking this, there was a commotion at our feet. The mottled dog was sniffing the hind section of the white dog, and the white dog was protesting.

Suddenly Jeremy started to singsong, "Gay dog; gay dog! Max's a gay dog!"

Now Max was trying to mount the other dog, and there was a toothy rebuff. Jeremy continued to sing, "Toby doesn't want him, but Max is in Love – Love – Love!"

I looked at Jake amazed. "A boy dog can love a boy dog? Really . . . ?"

Jake, a bit weird, said, "That one does." And then he added, "Let's go back outside."

So we ran, and the dogs followed after us in frolic.

Jeremy picked up his stick and beat at the strange tree again.

"What kind of tree is that?" I asked Jake quietly.

"Flo says it's from Australia – a cigar tree – because they used to smoke the long pods."

"Really?" I said in disbelief. "Smoke them?"

"Yeah, smoke them like cigars. She says down there it's called a 'F*g Tree.'"

"A f*g tree?" I said, thinking will the wonders of this day never end. "Why?"

Jake looked weird again; kinda sad. He glanced up into the branches, and I could sense a lie in his "I don't know."

I have to say, at that moment, looking at his profile tilted upwards and lost in his own thoughts, I have no idea why, but I knew I liked Jake. His brother was fun, wild; but in this kid two years my senior, I had met someone different from any of the boys in my class, perhaps more different than any boy I knew in school. Jake and I were alike. Liking him was like liking myself – the *Big I* put to peaceful rest.

As I was still thinking about him, Jake turned to look at the road. I did too. A tan boat of a Crown Victoria – same as Willetta's car – turned into the driveway.

"Jeremy!" Jake was now all business. "They're back!"

Jeremy dropped his stick and smoothed his shirt into his waistband.

The car pulled up to the screened-in porch and parked. A man got out and went around the front of the car, apparently not noticing us. He opened the passenger door and helped a woman out. The man had a short and shaggy beard with mustache the same color as the brothers' hair.

"Our folks," Jake said to me. There was something tense about the boys' father.

Together, their folks walked up to us.

"Who's this?" he asked Jake. There was no warmth in the question.

"Flo's friend. His name is Simon."

The man glanced at my dad's truck, then at and over me. "Don't call your grandmother 'Flo.' How old are you, son?" He meant me.

"Ten," I said.

"Your school?"

"Saint Lazarus."

"Oh . . . " He pursed his lips, drawing his face hair together for a moment to completely hide his mouth. He turned to his wife. "Catholic." She glanced at the ground. He pulled at his wife's elbow and walked to the house. "Not too much longer, boys – Jeremy; Jake." And before he went in, I saw Jake lower his eyes with one final, sharp, glance from his father. The dogs ran in with the older folks, and the screen door slammed behind them.

I couldn't help but swallow hard – it was like forcing something bitter into my gut, because it looked like Jake was afraid of this man.

"Simon . . . ?" I heard my father's voice. "Time to go." I could see Flo, Rex and him standing by the truck.

I screwed up my nerve, and said quietly to Jake, "I want to come back here. Do you think I can?"

Now Jake's half-smile came back. "Sure you can."

Flo had one more treat for us. Standing by the truck door, Flo said, "Do you want to see Rex happy?" She had asked this of me, so I nodded. "You ever see," she went on teasingly, "a dog smile?"

"No." And I hadn't.

"Sit, Rex."

He did.

She bent closer to his face and crooned, "Are you a happy boy? A happy fellow? Smile, Rex. Smile!" And the dog, with some head bows, suddenly parted lips, top and bottom, to show his pearlies, while all the time his tail was sweeping the gravel.

"We didn't teach him this. I suppose he just saw all the smiling folks around him and figured it was the way to show happiness."

One more wonder I thought as we rattled back over the two-ton bridge, as we drove along the base of the bluffs with willows and hickories, and with the rose-tinted twilight jostling to the west behind us flooding my face through the truck's side mirror. I couldn't help but smile. I was a happy boy indeed.

Miss Hill comes into the classroom. She'd long finished lunch, and watched the class at play for most of the break. She glances at me harshly, then sits at her desk to rattle papers. At them, she asks me:

"Learning your lesson?"

"Yes, Miss Hill." I was fooling no one. As I move my glance off of her, I follow the length of the shelf. First past the globe – two-hundred and six countries – because I once asked Miss Hill how many nations were on Earth, and she told me to count, and she would tell me if I got the right answer. I figured later, she had no idea herself. Then, my glance followed the same path to the statue of Mary. 'Still downcast?' I considered. 'What do You, Queen of Heaven, have to be worried about anyway?'

A quick glance up to the clock showed a pained, slow, red secondhand twitching; I still had six more minutes. And now, I wondered how last summer, so dazzling, so hopeful, turned out like this.

Part 6: Star Wars Cards and Kmart Queers

Bright summer Saturdays rolled past. I was able to convince my dad to drop me off at Flo's farm almost every weekend, and pick me up at the end of the day. As autumn rolled around, Rex was kidnapped. A neighbor reported a strange car stopping, getting Rex inside and driving away.

Mysteriously, a couple of miserable days later for Flo, she opened her door, and in walked Rex with wagging tail. Flo said it must have been his toothy smile that put the would-be stealers off from keeping him. Even bad guys sometimes know to do the right thing, and they brought Rex home.

"Look at what I got." I fished out a stack of cards from my pants pocket. Jeremy and I were lying on the floor of his and Jake's bedroom. A window, with a frilly yellow lace curtain, flapped periodically as a warm autumn breeze blew in before drifting out again through the open bedroom door to the landing and enclosed staircase. Above where Jeremy and I lay, the ceiling was papered with world maps from the folds of old *National Geographic* magazines, and models of airplanes floated and rode the window-stream on unseeable fishing line.

I went on with pride. "I got them from the McDonald's at Saint Clair Square."

Jake, sitting barefoot and in jean shorts on his bed, bent down to see my cards. I gave him half, then the other half to Jeremy.

"Whoa . . . !" Jeremy sputtered. "Cool!"

I bent close to see Jeremy looking at Princess Leia, which he flipped to Chewbacca.

Jake sat cross-legged at the edge of his bed, and I leaned in on his leg to see what he was looking at. He had Luke Skywalker. He asked me, "You got these at the Mall? At the McDonalds there . . . ?"

I explained knowingly, "You've got to buy a few happy meals, then you get the set."

"Neat!" Jeremy exclaimed, standing and switching fistfuls of cards with Jake. I lay back on the floor with hands proudly behind my head.

Jake rang out in hopeful expectation, "I know this Christmas, they're gonna have the best toys for this movie – I can't wait!"

"Did I ever tell you"—I savored the fact that I was about to drop a bombshell—"that I have the Eagle 1, from Space: 1999? At home?"

I sat up to see Jake and Jeremy look slack-jawed at each other. They had never met an only child like me.

"You must be rich!" Jeremy slammed me – the worst of accusations among us kids.

"My parents didn't buy it," I explained. "It was a gift from Willetta." And they let it go.

"Next time," Jake asked with intense sincerity, "will you bring it with you?"

"Okay," I said, and I meant it – if I could remember.

"Let's play Battleship," Jeremy said as he gathered my Star Wars cards and pressed them into my hands.

Jake scooted on his bed, propping his back against the wall, and I first noticed a bruise on his leg. I kneeled and saw a scratch on his neck, then more on his face. I asked low, as Jeremy was noisily tossing game boxes from out of their closet,

"What happened?" I motioned to his neck with mine as the example. "You all right?"

Jake stiffened; he paused. His eyes darted from the closet to me. He said, "It's nothing." I could see his throat tighten and swallow. "I'm all right." Then he did some kind of weird smile; it seemed warm, but kind of afraid too.

"Battleship!" Jeremy sang out, running over with the two bulky cases cradled in his arms. "Who's first?" He plopped down full force onto his knees and set the games on the floor by me.

"Simon is," Jake said.

"Red or blue?" Jeremy asked me.

"Blue," I said.

Jeremy spun my game around and I lay on my stomach as he unlatched the flap of his, and started sorting his pieces. We both organized them carefully and gave a signal that we were ready to begin playing in earnest competition. Jeremy mimicked my posture, and propped his head on his palms. His socked feet gyrated in the air over his head and gray corduroys.

Later, during the game, we started talking again.

"F-8," Jeremy said.

"Dang it!" I cried. "A second hit." Pause. "J-4."

"Miss-sss," Jeremy sputtered out to my face.

"You still think your dog is"—I went limp-wristed—"*that* way?"

"B-6," Jeremy said. "Yeah, nobody ever changes things like that . . . . "

"Miss. Well, I remember the first time I heard the words *f*g*, *f*gg*t*, *queer*. Um – C-2."

"Miss! Um – F-2."

"Darn!" I glared at him. Jeremy laughed theatrically, tossing his head back impossibly far and lolling it side to side.

"Second hit. I was at Kmart in Belleville. As usual, my mom sends me off to the toy department while she shops—"

"Number . . . ?"

"Um – D-8."

"OH – second hit."

"What did you say . . . ?" My hand to my ear.

"Second! Hit!" Pause. "B-6."

"Miss. And this kid starts hanging around with me. He's my age, but he kept saying I was a 'F*g.' I don't know what he means. Then he says 'You know, F*gg*t, Gay-Boy, Queer.' I never heard any of them, except Gay before. Funny, ain't it? – Um – I-2."

"Miss—"

Jake said, "What'd he tell you it means?"

" . . . E-3."

"Miss. A-7," I said.

"Damn! You sank my Battleship!"

I clapped in Jeremy's face. Suddenly Jake was serious. "Didn't you mind him calling you that?!"

I thought about it a second. I shrugged. "It's not nice, but he didn't know me, so it doesn't mean he really thought that. Maybe he said it to me 'cause everybody says it to him."

Jeremy laughed.

"Besides," I continued. "How does anybody know? What does it matter . . . ?"

"It don't matter if you know"—Jake was insistent—"it's just important that it doesn't seem so . . . . " He trailed off.

I could tell Jake was upset about something, so I changed the subject. "Your folks go to church on Sundays?" The game was over.

"Boy, do they!" Jeremy said. Then he added to his brother, "You want to play?" Jake shook his head no, looking at his hands. "Suit yourself." Jeremy and I packed up our pieces.

I asked Jake, "Catholic, or Lutheran?"

"Neither," Jake mumbled. I was confused; what other type was there?

Jeremy picked up the game cases and went to the closet. He turned around with a soccer ball and kneed it in the air a couple of times. He said to us, "Let's go out."

"Not me," Jake said. "You guys go."

I looked at Jeremy and shook my head; meaning I'd stay here with Jake. Jeremy nodded and ran out the bedroom door.

I stood up and looked to the spot on Jake's bed next to him. He glanced at me, then scooted over so I could sit like him, next to him.

After a pause, I asked, "So – what kind of church do they go to?"

"Evangelical."

"What?"

"Ee-Van– It's the kind of church where the Bible is most important. You can't join until you're grown up . . . then you get baptized."

"I was baptized."

"Not to them you weren't. They don't baptize children. They think if a kid dies, there's no hope; it goes straight to Hell."

I thought about it a second. "But we have Purgatory – or, is it Limbo? Anyway, if a baby dies, it goes there to wait for the resurrection. Why would God send a baby to Hell?! That's weird stuff."

"Well, not to them. Anyone dying before making a strong commitment to preach the Gospel to fellow sinners, and try to save souls as an adult, must go to Hell. Only grown-ups can be baptized and saved to go to Heaven."

After a pause, in which Jake looked at his hands a while, and I searched his profile, I asked, "You gonna get baptized?"

He set a sad look on me. "I don't think so."

" . . . Why not . . . ?"

"They don't want me."

" . . . What's wrong with them, that they don't want a neat guy like you . . . ?"

Jake swallowed hard. He lolled his gaze up to the maps, then back down to his hands now wrenching in his lap. "My dad says I ain't worthy – not the right kind."

I felt bad for him. "You don't believe in Hell, do you? I don't." It was an odd thing to say, but somehow it felt right.

"What?" Jake murmured.

"I mean"—I started and tried to smile at him—"if God is our Father, and down here we're supposed to believe that our folks can only love us – no matter what kind of trouble we get into – then how can our Heavenly Father be any less for-giving than our parents? He should be more so. That's why I don't believe God can send anybody to Hell, 'cause, he doesn't hate anybody."

Now I did go too far. It seemed instead of distracting Jake from his problems, I worsened them. He gulped a choking sob into his throat, and an unwiped tear fell fast along his reddening cheek. His hands stopped their torment, and the one closest to me reached out to take mine, but he stopped. He blinked at me, more tears fell, and he looked miserable beyond words.

"What's wrong?" I took his hand. I squeezed it. I shook it a little, begging him to be honest. "You can tell me."

"You're too good to understand – your father is nice."

I was confused. We were talking about my dad? About Jake's dad? I was lost.

Suddenly, noiselessly, we looked up to the door. Jake's father was there and watching us. Jake jerked his hand out of mine and with it wiped his tears and snorted up his newly runny nose. His dad said to me, "Run along now, Simon. Your father is waiting for you." And he disappeared as quietly behind the doorframe as he had appeared.

Somehow the ride home seemed twice as long that evening. With each passing milepost glinting the setting sun behind us, I felt I should be moving back to where I started. I didn't want to leave Jake that evening – though he didn't ask; though he couldn't ask anything of me – it seemed stronger and stronger that he, my one true and closest friend, needed something from me. I didn't know what – protection? How could that be? After all, I'm just a kid – and so is he.

Part 7: The F*g Tree

Fall drifted into winter. Because of icy roads, I saw Jeremy and his brother less. I know they got Star Wars fighter toys and action figures for Christmas, because we played with them in their room. They were a gift from Flo. This happened over a visit after New Years, and that reminded me that I had never brought my Space: 1999 Eagle 1 for them to see. I heard they were taking a family trip to Disney World, and I was jealous as heck. But spring came, and I pressured by dad to restart our Saturday schedule. He acted odd though. Like he knew something I didn't. Like he was told something by Jake's dad, though I didn't know what. Maybe that I was a pest; it wouldn't be the first time for that! But spring pushed me, and I pushed him.

The Saturday after my encounter with Ralph in the vestry, and my talk with Monsignor Helfgott at his dining room table, I felt I needed to see Jake. Begging my dad, he agreed to go out to Flo's, but when I got there, Jeremy looked surprised to see me at the screened-in porch door. He let me in, but hushed me, as if I were in a sick house.

Creeping up the carpeted stairs, I could see the door to their room was closed. Halfway up, Jeremy stopped and turned to me with hoarse whispers.

"Jake's not supposed to see—" A word was missing. "He's not feeling too good. Don't let my folks see you with him – okay?"

"Why?"

"Don't ask"—he sighed, confessing—"because, my dad don't want you around us anymore. But, I know . . . " he said looking at the door. "That's not fair to Jake."

"I don't understand."

"Look – all right? My dad and Jake don't get along. Last time – that time he saw you guys together, alone – Jake got it pretty bad. But after that it just got worse. This week, Jake had to miss some school . . . " He was very earnest now. "Look, that's a family secret, okay? You're not gonna tell anyone – right?"

I was stunned.

" . . . Yeah; but, no. But, what about your mom? What about Flo?"

Jeremy looked like he hated to tell me. "They know, somehow, but they act like there's nothing they can do about it. Understand?"

I didn't. I swallowed hard. There was a sinking nausea down there, and I thought maybe it was best for me to go, but I had to know, "What did we do? What did I do?"

Jeremy blinked in surprise. Matter-of-factly he told me, "Nothing. You did nothing; he did nothing. It's just – my dad and Jake don't get along. That's all." Jeremy's shield was still up, but as he took a step, he sighed and was honest with me. "He don't want Jake to be *that* way. It's against God, he says. He wants Jake to snap out of it, even if my dad has to whoop it out of him, before it's too late." Jeremy turned to go up. I grabbed his arm and stopped him.

"Do you think he is?"

"I think I don't care. He's my brother either way. That means I love him, either way."

I went into their room alone. I closed the door behind me. Jake was lying on top of his sheets. He was wearing a navy tank top with red edging and white shorts. His eyes were closed, and I wasn't prepared to see his face with cuts and a bruised eye. His arms were bruised black on the inside of his biceps, and something like kick marks were healing on his shins.

He opened his eyes and sat up with a pained grimace.

I sat on the floor in front of him. I started telling him slowly, "I'm sorry to hear you're not feeling well."

" . . . Thanks . . . . "

After a pause, I asked, "You want to do something?" Then I remembered Jeremy's warning. "I mean, we can play a game"—I was looking around—"here, in your room."

"No." Jake stood up. I could see he was in pain, so I got up to help him. He tossed back a gulp of air, steeling his nerves before he told me, "I've got to tell you something – but not here."

Again, I stood at the top of the landing within Flo's loft. Again, it was dark, and again magic flooded out as Jake flipped the light switch.

I couldn't help but smile, and when Jake saw me, for the first time in what seemed a long time, I saw his face lighten too.

We walked around, poking fingers in and out of fancy carved table supports, and across the tops of counters and glass cases. At an area where a bit of clearing formed, Jake sat down with outstretched legs. He leaned his back against a display cabinet. The lights from inside gave a halo to his chestnut hair. I sat cross-legged in front of him. I tried to smile. I asked, "So, what do you want to tell me?"

Jake's grin was gone. It looked like I was killing him. "We took our trip to Disney World—"

"I know; lucky jerk."

"—And it turns out, my dad found a lot of churches . . . " There was a fleeting meeting of my gaze. "You know – his type of church . . . " His eyes returned to watch his hands. "And, they've decided to move to Florida. We're going to drive down in a couple of weeks."

"Florida?" Saying it made me feel sick; no place ever sounded so far away. Grasping at straws, I blurted, "But you'll be back to visit your grandma! Right . . . ?"

Jake held my eyes, and lied. "Yeah."

"Well"—now I sighed—"we'll see each other then."

" . . . Maybe . . . . "

I just then remembered. "I brought my camera today. Remember, I told you, the Kodak that takes Polaroids? I got it for Christmas."

"Oh. Good."

Trying to be cheery, I added, "I brought lots of film, so we can each keep some copies—"

I was interrupted because loud sobs began to come out of Jake's mouth and throat. I reached out a hand and put it on his forearm. He jerked it away.

"It's gonna be all right," I said. "Everything will work out, in the end; it always does."

His eyes looking everywhere but me, he choked out, "Why does my dad hate me?"

I got to my knees and crawled over to Jake's case. I copied him, and leaned my back against the lit glass by his side. He had drawn up his knees and raised his elbows on them. Now he only stared at the floor in front of his feet. I blinked in some earnest wish to make everything all right with Jake, so I lifted my arm and rested my hand across his back on his far shoulder. I was about to mouth a conventional 'He doesn't hate you,' but we were clearly beyond that point. For once it was time to cut all the malarkey. It was time for one person to listen and to hear, really hear, so that two could connect in honesty.

I finally said, "I don't know why he hates you. No father has any right to hate his kids." I tried to chuckle, and failed. "But, why let it get you down? It's totally his loss."

I had to stop a moment, because it was true. I knew Jake was a great guy. I couldn't understand how anybody, least of all his folks, could feel any different.

"*If* he hates you," I continued, "it's because he won't let himself *see* you. He takes what he wants to see – maybe what he wants, doesn't want to see in himself – and tries to fit it onto you. Maybe his mistakes make him worry about you. But"—I gripped his shoulder harder—"we're just kids! What do we know? Only that our parents should love us, and should protect us. But, if he won't, to hell with him. Who needs him? That's why we've got brothers, right? That's why we've got friends."

There was a long pause. My hand felt funny, and heavy, on his unresponsive shoulder, so I pulled it away. I finally asked, "You gonna run away?"

"No."

"It might be best, you know, if—"

"I can't."

"Why not? If it's not safe for you—"

He cut me off again. "I can't, because — I've got to protect Jeremy."

For the life of me, I couldn't puzzle out how that was an answer to my question. But, I nodded, and couldn't stop myself from asking, "Protect him . . . from what . . . ? Jeremy and your dad don't get along either?"

Jake looked shocked. "You are too good. You . . . you, just don't get it, do you?"

I shrugged. "I might be able to."

"I keep my dad off of Jeremy. If I'm not there—" Jake couldn't go on. Was that . . . shame on Jake's face? That look — the same as on Ralph, the same as on the Monsignor — sent a cold shiver down my back. I did not understand. Jake hadn't done anything; that much I knew.

To hell with it, I put my hand back across his back. I rocked Jake a quiet moment, trying to get him to cheer up, and then, as softly as I could, I added, "So, who cares if you're Gay—"

Jake pushed me back, toppling my shoulder to the floor. He stood and bent a mean glare down on me. His fist drew back in full anger to punch me. "I ain't no F*gg*t!" he said, and spittle stung my eyes. I thought he would hit me, but after another moment, he stumbled backwards a couple of paces like a drunk on TV.

I stood myself up. I stood myself up to him. I really didn't care if he wanted to hit me. If his dad had hit him because of me, then somehow it seemed only fair that Jake sock me one for it.

"Okay!" I said, half-reaching for his forearm. "So you ain't. So your dad's a big fat jerk. So you feel like shit 'cause he treats you like shit. I bet he's just like that kid in Kmart — he says it to others cause he hears it a lot, or heard it a lot when he was your age. Maybe he can't help but pass it along . . . but

– you missed my point. My point is – who cares? Who cares if a girl loves a girl, or a boy a boy – what difference does it make?"

"Difference!" he shouted, knocking my arm back. "It's the difference between love and hate; that's all! Between life and death . . . that's . . . all—" Suddenly, his fury was spent. He pleadingly locked onto my gaze. "Not even you can be too good to understand the difference between living and dying. Like love and hate, we usually don't get to choose which."

I didn't know what to say. Jake pushed past me. He moved away, over to a cabinet full of porcelain children with rose swags and trees with swings. After a long moment, Jake murmured something down to them, and I had to go up behind him to hear.

"You want to know the truth . . . ?" he repeated.

"About what?"

"Why they call it a F*g Tree?"

"Okay, yes."

"My dad says it's called that, because down in Australia, it's the tree they used to hang guys like me. He says, one day, he'll string me up there himself."

I put my fist into his hand from behind and forced him to turn to me. I wasn't giving up on Jake. "Why do you care what your dad thinks? You ain't; you ain't. You are; you are – to hell with him – you're the one that matters."

"I care because he says God doesn't want me like that."

"But," I said and blinked, because this seemed obvious to me, "it's God that makes people. He doesn't make mistakes. However the way you are, the way any of us are, it's because God wants us that way."

Jake seemed confused. But soon his darting expression settled into something that looked like relief.

I squeezed his hand and then shook it up to his shoulder. "Right?" I asked. "Right!" I demanded.

He let out a long breath he'd been hiding from me. I felt his hand grip mine in return.

"Right," he said.

I led Jake back over to the case we had been leaning on. I made him sit. I sat and put my arm around him.

"Think of all the fun you'll have in Florida. I wish I was going! You'll get to go to Disney World *every* day – you'll get to swim with Flipper . . . " Now I was excited. "You'll love it . . . !"

But Jake looked worse yet. He propped the back of his head on the cabinet, and again a tear went from the corner of his eye and fell slowly into the corner of his mouth.

"Don't worry," I whispered. "Things will get better with your old man. Down there, things will change. I just know it. You wait and see."

Jake reached up and put both arms around me. I felt his wild tears on my cheek. As he sobbed, his were joined with mine.

"I'm gonna miss you," he choked out.

For some reason, I lifted my hand. I stroked the haloed chestnut hair of this boy two years older than me as if he were an infant. I soothed it over and over again as he cried, and I tried to say "I'm gonna miss you too" but, I don't think anything came out.

In my dad's truck, as we rolled away from the twilight, I held up a Polaroid square. In the breeze that flapped in from the black farm soil beyond, I looked at Jake and me standing arm in arm. Flo had rustled us up against the side of her barn, by the living room, and set Rex to sit at our touching feet. "Smile!" she had called out – and Jake, and me, we couldn't smile – how? – it seemed all of humanity in the two of us had never smiled before in our lives. For Jake and me it was an impossible request. For us, the act of holding on was enough – more than enough. But for Rex, the familiar command caused him on cue, no doubt because he was happy, to bare his teeth and brush the grass with his tail.

In the rose-colored light coming from behind me, Jeremy had gone into a half-gig, half-lightsaber parry when I lowered the tailgate of my dad's truck and pulled a box forward. Jake and Jeremy peered at my Space: 1999 Eagle 1, and I said, "You guys can keep it." And then quietly to Jake, I added, "Just don't forget me."

And now, rolling homeward, this picture – one snap-shot – was my last tangible link to the first person I knew in my heart, without any doubt, was a true friend to me. My only consolation was in thinking that Jake too had a near-identical snapshot, and maybe, he wouldn't forget me after all.

Part 8: Mary on Top of the World

The school bell rings loudly and sharply. Lunch break is over. Miss Hill comes up to me and takes the books, and then half-sneers, "Well, did you think about what has happened?"

I collapse into my desk chair, my eyes lighting on the pitiless, pained look, on the face of the 4th grade Madonna.

"Yes," I said, as she puts the books back in order on the shelf.

My classmates stream in, laughing; chatting merrily about many nothings. And my mind's eye shifts out to the school's lobby. While the statue of Mary is different in each class – the 2nd grade one even has blond hair – the power-force of Saint Lazarus School Marys is the life-size one in the lobby corner. Here, her black hair pours out from beneath a sky-blue veil to fall over shoulders, and then down to her bent elbows, which end by coming forward with her hands locking in prayer. Her violet eyes cast gazes over all of us children who pass beneath her perch on the North Pole – America front and center, with her gold sandals crushing the Canadian prairie lands. But this Mary looks sadder than all the rest. This Mary wears a starry crown; this Mary treads on a green serpent. It writhes its way from coast to coast, and I suppose, the devil himself is ground under her heel. Yet, if she has so much power over evil, why does she cast such remorseful eyes on the children she watches? Where is evil? – In the devil's heart, or, in our own? Where is betrayal? – In the garden's temptation? Or, in the Judas kiss? And love? – In a helpless standing-by? Or, in Judas defiling the priests' eternal home?

Perhaps I was wrong to tell Jake to stick to a family situation where he was an outsider. I wanted to believe what I told him – that things will get better – but I should have told him then what I thought of later. That dealing with his dad takes all the skill and planning that Jake and Jeremy use on their fan. The right approach; the correct application of force, on the right spot, and the cutting blades of his quarrels with his son would stop – would be forced to stop. Somehow though, I think I said as much to Jake without needing to spell it out. Jake knows what to do. Maybe that's why I feel so strongly that things will get better for him – because he will know just how to make them better – even if he does have to run away, and find a new family.

And what of our hallway Madonna? Is there any safety in her powerless pity, or merely opportunity for the worst of human instincts to let things pass by, under voiceless sorrow – and how am I to know? I am just a kid.

I pull out my math book. Miss Hill starts the lesson, and a sinking feeling of being sick settles down my throat.

Yes, I had thought about what had happened, and I had swallowed hard. For what in the whole world is worse than a father not loving a son; a mother not loving a daughter; or God not loving all of us enough to keep us safe.

Outside these walls, the spring air forms swirling eddies to shake the boughs of the trees nearby. I can see them. I can sense them –

The Judas tree stands for frailty and blood-remorse. The treachery of trust itself wracks its weak branches, and guilt stains it blossoms.

The spruce is a tower of respectability – but sticky, it traps innocence with sharp needles that bear neither fruit nor flower.

The cigar tree – the F*g tree – it weeps like a willow for all those who have gone before, but it is stately. It holds its head up high, no matter what.

As I turn the page, I hope I am not about to stain it. I feel now that any betrayal of love is a betrayal of God, and worthy of action to see right done; to do right; and create right in the name of whatever is good here on Earth – the only place He has given us to live, to love, and where we all must eventually die.

I swallow hard again. This time I can taste it. This time, I know what it is I am putting into my gut. It is anger. I am angry.